HANSEL AND GRETEL

WRITTEN BY
THE BROTHERS GRIMM

RETOLD AND ILLUSTRATED BY
RACHEL ISADORA

G. P. PUTNAM'S SONS

Once there lived a poor woodcutter who had come upon hard times. He could no longer feed his wife and children.

"Tomorrow we will take the children deep into the forest and there we will leave them," said the children's stepmother.

"I cannot do that to my own children," the man said.

"If you don't, then all four of us will starve," said the wife, and she gave him no peace until he agreed.

Hansel and Gretel had overheard what their stepmother said.

"Don't worry. I know what to do," said Hansel. As soon as the adults fell asleep, Hansel crept outside and filled his pockets with pebbles.

The next morning the stepmother woke Hansel and Gretel.
She told them that they were going to collect wood and gave them
each a small piece of bread.

As they walked, Hansel kept stopping. "What are you doing?"
his father asked.

"I'm looking at my cat sitting on our roof," Hansel said.

"You fool, that is just the morning sun shining on the chimney,"
the stepmother scolded.

But Hansel had not been looking at his cat. He had been dropping
pebbles onto the path.

When they were deep in the forest, their father said, "You children gather wood and I will make a fire so you won't freeze." When the fire was lit, the stepmother told the children to wait while she and their father went to cut more wood.

Hansel and Gretel ate their bread and waited. But no one came to get them. When it grew dark, Gretel began to cry. "Don't worry," Hansel said.

The pebbles Hansel had dropped
glistened in the moonlight, and the
children followed them home. When
their father saw them, he was overjoyed.
The stepmother pretended that she was
happy too, but secretly she was angry.

Not long afterward, Hansel and Gretel
heard the stepmother tell their father,
"We again have very little food, so we
must be rid of the children."

When their parents were asleep, Hansel
went to gather pebbles, but this time the door
had been locked by the stepmother.

In the morning, the stepmother gave Hansel and
Gretel even smaller pieces of bread, which Hansel
secretly dropped as they walked along the path.

Now the children were left
even deeper in the forest. Once
again they waited by a fire, but no
one came to get them. As it grew darker,
Gretel began to cry.

"Don't worry. The moonlight will shine
on the pieces of bread and we will find
our way home," Hansel said.
But when they looked for
the bread, they realized
that it had been eaten
by the birds.

For three days Hansel and Gretel tried to find their way out
of the forest. They were terribly hungry when they came to
a little house built entirely from bread with a roof made of cake
and windows made of sugar. They began to gobble down pieces
of the house when they heard a voice calling from inside:

"Nibble, nibble, little mouse,
Who is nibbling at my house?"

Suddenly, the door opened and out came an old woman. Hansel and Gretel were so frightened, they dropped what they were eating.

But the old lady said, "Oh, you dear children. Come inside with me and you will be just fine." She served them a delicious meal, and Hansel and Gretel went to sleep thinking they were in heaven.

But the woman only pretended to be friendly. She was really a wicked witch who built her sweet house in order to tempt children and capture them for a tasty meal.

While Hansel and Gretel slept,
the witch looked at them. "They
will be a good mouthful," she said.
In the morning she grabbed Hansel
and locked him in a cage. She ordered
Gretel to cook for her brother so
he could be fattened up.

Every day the witch said to Hansel, "Stick out your finger so I can feel if you are fat enough."

But the witch had bad eyes, so Hansel would stick out a little bone that Gretel gave him. The witch wondered why he wasn't getting any fatter.

The witch grew hungrier and hungrier and finally she could wait no longer. She told Gretel to fetch water in which her brother was to be boiled while she made bread.

Then she told Gretel to go climb inside the oven to see if it was hot enough. But Gretel could see that the witch planned to bake her, so she said, "I don't know how. Show me."

"Stupid goose, the opening is big enough. I could get in myself," the witch cackled as she stuck her head into the oven. Quickly Gretel gave the witch a big shove and pushed her all the way inside.

While the witch burned, Gretel ran and unlocked Hansel's cage.

Hansel and Gretel jumped for joy and filled their pockets with the witch's precious stones and pearls. When they found their way back home, their father rejoiced to see them, for he had not had a happy day since they had been gone. During their time away, their stepmother had died. Now all their cares were at an end, and they lived happily together.

My tale is done,

A mouse has run.

And whoever catches it can make for himself

from it a large, large fur cap.

For my G and N

G. P. PUTNAM'S SONS
A division of Penguin Young Readers Group.
Published by The Penguin Group.
Penguin Group (USA) Inc., 375 Hudson Street, New York, NY 10014, U.S.A.
Penguin Group (Canada), 90 Eglinton Avenue East, Suite 700, Toronto, Ontario M4P 2Y3, Canada
(a division of Pearson Penguin Canada Inc.).
Penguin Books Ltd, 80 Strand, London WC2R 0RL, England.
Penguin Ireland, 25 St. Stephen's Green, Dublin 2, Ireland (a division of Penguin Books Ltd.).
Penguin Group (Australia), 250 Camberwell Road, Camberwell, Victoria 3124, Australia (a division of Pearson Australia Group Pty Ltd).
Penguin Books India Pvt Ltd, 11 Community Centre, Panchsheel Park, New Delhi - 110 017, India.
Penguin Group (NZ), 67 Apollo Drive, Rosedale, North Shore 0632, New Zealand (a division of Pearson New Zealand Ltd).
Penguin Books (South Africa) (Pty) Ltd, 24 Sturdee Avenue, Rosebank, Johannesburg 2196, South Africa.
Penguin Books Ltd, Registered Offices: 80 Strand, London WC2R 0RL, England.

Manufactured in China by RR Donnelley Asia Printing Solutions Ltd.
Design by Marikka Tamura. Text set in Geist.
The illustrations were done with oil paints, printed paper and palette paper.
Library of Congress Cataloging-in-Publication Data.
Isadora, Rachel. Hansel and Gretel / written by the Brothers Grimm ; retold and illustrated by Rachel Isadora. p. cm.
Summary: When they are left in the woods by their parents, two children find their way home despite an encounter
with a wicked witch. [1. Fairy tales. 2. Folklore—Germany.] I. Grimm, Jacob, 1785–1863. II. Grimm, Wilhelm, 1786–1859.
III. Hansel and Gretel. English. IV. Title. PZ8.I84Han 2009 398.2—dc22 [E] 2008018580
ISBN 978-0-399-25028-6
10